Jack trailed off as he glanced round to find that Victoria had disappeared.

'Where's she gone to?' he asked, puzzled. 'She was standing there only a minute ago.'

'Bet she nipped off quick, like, so she don't 'ave to carry 'owt,' Harry cackled. 'C'mon, let's do the same.'

They left the park at a steady jog but the only ones to catch sight of the mysterious new striker were Amy and Ellie. The girls reached the playground just in time to see Victoria enter the building site. To their utter astonishment, she seemed to pass right through the safety fence, drift over the mounds of rubble and then fade from view.

An icy shiver snaked down Ellie's spine. 'Where . . . where did she go?'

Amy was in no state to reply. She stood rooted to the spot, open-mouthed, gawping at the empty space where Victoria had vanished.

Also available by Rob Childs,
published by Corgi Yearling Books

County Cup series
1: CUP FAVOURITES
2: CUP RIVALS
3: CUP SHOCKS
4: CUP CLASHES
5:CUP GLORY
6: CUP FEVER
7: CUP WINNERS

Soccer Mad series
FOOTBALL FANATIC
SOCCER MAD
ALL GOALIES ARE CRAZY
FOOTBALL DAFT
FOOTBALL FLUKES
SOCCER STARS
SOCCER SHOCKS

THE SOCCER MAD COLLECTION
includes Soccer Mad and All Goalies Are Crazy

THE SOCCER MAD DOUBLE
includes Football Daft and Football Flukes

Published by Young Corgi Books:

THE BIG BREAK
THE BIG CHANCE
THE BIG CLASH
THE BIG DAY
THE BIG DROP
THE BIG FIX
THE BIG FREEZE
THE BIG GAME

THE BIG GOAL
THE BIG KICK
THE BIG MATCH
THE BIG PRIZE
THE BIG SEND-OFF
THE BIG STAR
THE BIG TIME
THE BIG WIN

THE BIG FOOTBALL COLLECTION
includes The Big Game, The Big Match and The Big Prize

THE BIG FOOTBALL FEAST
includes The Big Day, The Big Kick and The Big Goal

THE BIG FOOTBALL TREBLE
includes The Big Break, The Big Chance and The Big Star

THE BIG FOOTBALL FRENZY
includes The Big Freeze, The Big Win and The Big Fix

Published by Corgi Pups Books,
for beginner readers:

GREAT SAVE!
GREAT SHOT!
GREAT HIT!
GREAT GOAL!

ROB CHILDS

TEAM SPIRIT

**ILLUSTRATED BY
JERRY PARIS**

CORGI YEARLING BOOKS

TEAM SPIRIT
A CORGI YEARLING BOOK : 0 440 864046

First publication in Great Britain

PRINTING HISTORY
Corgi Yearling edition published 2001

1 3 5 7 9 10 8 6 4 2

Set in 12/15pt Century Schoolbook by
Falcon Oast Graphic Art

Corgi Books are published by Transworld Publishers,
61–63 Uxbridge Road, London W5 5SA
a division of The Random House Group Ltd,
in Australia by Random House Australia (Pty) Ltd,
20 Alfred Street, Milsons Point, Sydney, NSW 2061, Australia,
in New Zealand by Random House New Zealand Ltd,
18 Poland Road, Glenfield, Auckland 10, New Zealand
and in South Africa by Random House (Pty) Ltd,
Endulini, 5a Jubilee Road, Parktown 2193, South Africa.

Made and printed in Great Britain by
Cox & Wyman Ltd, Reading, Berkshire

TEAM SPIRIT

1 SOCCER MAD

'D'yer reckon he might?'

'No 'arm in askin', eh?'

'So who's gonna ask him, then?'

The boys' discussion had rambled on like this ever since they'd been forced to abandon their lunchtime kickabout. The ball had gone out of bounds into an area fenced off from the playground while building work was in progress. Their school, dating back to Victorian times, was having a new library and computer block built to mark its 150th anniversary.

'What you all looking at me for?' demanded Jack.

'Well, old Stampy knows you're our best player,' said Owen, hoping that a touch of flattery might help.

'And 'cos 'e likes you,' put in Harry.

'I'm no teacher's pet,' Jack snarled.

'Never said yer were. It's just that, y'know, old Stampy used to teach yer brother – and yer mam.'

Jack bristled even more. 'What's that got to do with it?'

'Well, nothin',' he confessed. 'But, I mean, like, y'know . . .'

Harry dried up. He'd already dug a hole for himself deeper than any in the building site. He needed some help to climb out and Callum eventually came to his pal's rescue.

'What we're really sayin', Jack, is that old Stampy might listen to you more than any of us,' he explained. 'You don't try and work *well, y'know, like, I mean* into every sentence!'

'That's what I meant, like, y'know,' Harry said lamely.

Jack gave a shrug. 'Anyway, he'll probably say no, just like Freddie.'

'But he's not like Freddie, is he?' Owen argued. 'She hates football.'

'OK,' Jack sighed. 'Just let me try and choose the right time.'

'Gotta be today, like,' said Harry. 'I mean, Freddie's back tomorrow.'

'Yeah, but I bet she'll be away again soon,' Owen grinned. 'She loves going on courses.'

'Must be better than tryin' to teach us lot!' laughed Callum.

Whenever Mrs Fredericks was absent, Mr Stamp, a former teacher at Bradgate Junior School, was called in to take her place. The children were always glad to see him. He didn't work them so hard and often finished a session with a short story or a few funny poems.

The bell rang for the end of lunchtime and the boys wandered across the playground towards the two-storey brick building.

'So are yer gonna ask 'im s'afto, like?' Harry persisted.

Jack nodded. 'Guess so. If only to stop you lot nagging me.'

The timing appeared to be perfect. After clearing up from a messy art and craft lesson, Mr Stamp read the class part of a soccer story.

'What did you think of it?' he asked, closing the book.

Amy's hand shot up first.

'Yes . . . um . . . ?' he faltered, looking her way.

'Amy, Mr Stamp,' she said, knowing that his memory for names was not exactly one of the teacher's strengths.

'So what were you going to say, Amy?'

'Well, I suppose it was all right, Mr Stamp, but there were no girls in it.'

Several of the boys turned to pull faces at her, but she ignored them.

'Good point, Amy,' Mr Stamp conceded. 'I'm afraid this story was written before girls were allowed to play football in school teams.'

'They still can't here,' she said cheekily.

'We don't even have a team!'

'No, that's a pity,' he replied. 'You like playing football, do you?'

'Don't get the chance,' Amy grumbled. 'Mrs Fredericks makes all us girls do netball instead.'

'And which position do you play in netball?'

'Shooter – I like scoring goals!'

Jack sensed several pairs of eyes drilling into him, expecting him to speak. He raised his hand.

'Yes, Jack?' said Mr Stamp. 'Have you got something to say on this subject or are you referring to the story?'

'Well, like . . .'

'Huh! He's startin' to sound like me,' Harry grunted.

'It's just that we were wondering,' Jack continued, finally getting into his stride, 'if the school might be able to have a football team again?'

'Why are you asking me?' Mr Stamp said. 'I've retired now. Isn't there anyone on the staff who might be interested?'

He knew the answer to that himself.

Jack shook his head. 'They say they haven't

13

time – and that we've got nowhere to play with having no school field,' he said. 'But when my brother was here, you used to have matches on the park.'

'Times have changed, unfortunately,' Mr Stamp admitted. 'There isn't even a pitch marked out there any more.'

'You could ask to get one done,' Callum piped up eagerly.

'Whoa! Hold your horses,' the teacher chuckled. 'I'm not sure if I want to get involved in all that sort of thing again. I did it for so many years – and in all kinds of weather. I remember one game played in several inches of snow. Must have been mad in my younger days.'

'Soccer mad!' cackled Harry.

'Aye, well, you could be right there, lad,' he smiled, happy to reminisce about some of his funny experiences in the past – if only to avoid responding to the original enquiry about a new school team.

He was also saved by the bell.

'I don't know,' he sighed when the children had gone home. 'I really would be mad if I started up all that lark again at my age.'

 14

Mr Stamp wandered over to gaze out of the window, high up on the second floor, and his attention was caught by a tiny, red-haired figure down on the playground below.

It – she – was kicking a ball against a wall, using both feet. The girl showed considerable skill, both in ball control and the accuracy of her shooting into a roughly chalked goal on the brickwork.

'Good little player, by the look of it,' he mused. 'Perhaps that Amy has a point. Girls *can* play football. Don't recognize her, though. Wonder who she is?'

Mr Stamp felt drawn to go and find out. He left the classroom and went down the main staircase, but by the time he emerged into the playground it was deserted. The girl was nowhere to be seen.

15

2 WHO WANTS TO PLAY?

Mr Stamp was called back into school mid-way through the following week, but not to replace Mrs Fredericks. He came in to cover for another teacher who had fallen ill.

He also found that he was expected to do her turn on duty at morning break. It was a chilly, autumnal day, with the buffeting wind creating whirlpools of paper and leaves in every corner of the playground.

'Typical!' he grunted as he stood on the steps of the building, huddled into his overcoat and cradling a cup of tea which was rapidly cooling. 'People always seem to be away when it's their duty day.'

Out of habit, Mr Stamp watched the hustle and bustle of the main game of football, mostly involving the older boys. He knew that anyone younger who was allowed to join in would have needed to prove their worth. Bearing in mind Jack's request, he studied the talent on view with an experienced eye.

He wasn't too impressed – and nor were two other spectators.

'Not much cop, are they, Mr Stamp.'

It was more of a statement than a question, but it needed some kind of response. The teacher found two girls by his side.

'Oh, hello again . . .' he began.

'Ellie and Amy – in Mrs Fredericks' class,' prompted the taller one with black ringlets of hair. 'And I'm Ellie.'

'Ah, yes, right,' he murmured. 'You think you could do better, then, the pair of you?'

'We couldn't do much worse,' Amy answered, pulling a face. 'But they won't even let us play.'

 18

'Bet they're scared we might show 'em up,' Ellie laughed.

'Do you want to play?' asked Mr Stamp, grinning.

Amy shrugged, her usual response to a direct question. 'Yeah, maybe.'

'No use askin', though,' said Ellie. 'Waste of breath.'

'Well, I won't ask, then,' he said. 'I'll just tell them.'

Before the girls could respond, or even try to stop him, Mr Stamp called out to Jack who had just barged past an opponent and lobbed the ball towards goal for others to fight over.

'Got two more players for you, Jack.'

Jack checked around in vain. 'Where, Mr Stamp?'

'Here,' he chuckled, enjoying the boy's confusion. Jack had ignored the girls completely. 'Amy and Ellie.'

Jack looked blank, as if he still hadn't quite taken in the situation.

'One on each side,' Mr Stamp added. 'That's fair, isn't it?'

'Who's winning?' asked Amy, stepping forward.

'We are, 3–1,' Jack muttered.

'Right, I'll be on your side,' she decided. 'The other lot can have Ellie.'

'Oh, thanks a bunch,' Ellie sneered.

Mr Stamp forgot all about the cold dregs of his tea, focusing his attention on the game. It soon became clear, however, that the boys had no intention of passing the ball to either of the girls.

'Right, if that's the way you want to play, I'll get it myself,' Amy said under her breath.

The next time the ball came accidentally in her direction, she swooped over to whisk it off a boy's toes.

'Hey! You're on my team,' he shouted as she dribbled the ball away.

'Too late,' Amy cackled. Now that she had possession at last, she intended to make the most of it.

 2

Callum made no attempt to win the ball back cleanly. He barged into Amy from behind and knocked her off balance. She almost fell over, a tumble that usually resulted in a grazed arm on the concrete. Amy somehow kept her feet, but not the ball, which ran loose as she staggered into the wall.

'Foul!' she cried. 'That was a dirty, deliberate foul.'

'Prove it!' Callum jeered. 'There's no ref.'

Mr Stamp was tempted to intervene but wisely decided not to. It wouldn't have done Amy any favours if the teacher had to come to her rescue. Besides, he felt that she was perfectly capable of looking after herself.

He was right. Amy was soon throwing herself into the thick of the action, using her speed to good effect to keep out of any further trouble and to enable her to have the occasional kick of the ball.

Mr Stamp smiled when he guessed that the ball was not the only thing that she kicked. As Callum challenged strongly for possession in a crowded goalmouth, he received a painful blow on the knee.

Amy protested her innocence. 'Don't blame

 21

me,' she snapped when he complained. 'I wasn't anywhere near you!'

Ellie was not quite so involved in the game, preferring to stay back in defence and wait for the ball to come her way. Her one moment of glory came when she was in position to clear the ball to safety after goalkeeper Harry was beaten. He had no intention of diving on the hard surface.

'Cheers, Ellie!' he cried. 'Good block, that.'

It was the only praise either of the girls received for their efforts, but Mr Stamp judged that they had not looked out of place. When he rang the bell to signal the end of break, the girls trotted towards him to collect their coats from the steps.

'Well done, both of you,' said the teacher. 'I think you might have proved a point or two there.'

'Um, Mr Stamp . . .' Amy began tentatively. 'If you did decide to run a school team, it *would* be mixed, wouldn't it?'

He chuckled. 'I'm sure it would. From what I've seen here, these lads will need a bit of help from some of you girls, even if they won't admit it.'

 22

His memory was jogged of the little girl he'd seen kicking a ball about in the playground after school.

'By the way,' he said, 'do you know the name of another girl I saw playing football last week? Quite small, she was, with reddish hair.'

Amy shook her head. 'Don't know anyone like that, do you, Ellie?'

Ellie shrugged. 'There's them sisters with ginger hair in the lower juniors, but I don't think they're any good with a ball.'

'Hmm, right,' he replied, puzzled. 'Perhaps I'll check it out myself later.'

Unfortunately Mr Stamp had neither the time nor the opportunity to do so. As soon as he walked back into the classroom he was besieged by questions, and all thoughts of the mystery girl flew out of his mind.

Before he left for home that day, he pinned up a notice in the main corridor. It offered children the chance to sign their names if they were interested in attending a soccer practice. So many of them had asked him about it by now that he had finally given in.

'I must need my head examining,' he sighed as he trudged wearily down the staircase, glad at least that he wasn't required to teach the next day.

Mr Stamp didn't return, in fact, until a fortnight later. He could hardly believe his eyes when he checked the noticeboard. The original sheet of paper was so full of names that another piece had been added for other people to write theirs, including a number of girls.

His attention was caught by a neatly printed name right at the bottom of the list, but the handwriting was so small that he had to put on his glasses to read it more easily.

'Victoria Bradgate,' he murmured. 'That's odd, having the same name as the school. Wonder which class she's in?'

He folded the sheets and tucked them away into his jacket pocket, not realizing that the question would have been better phrased in the past tense.

3 MYSTERY GIRL

The following Wednesday afternoon, Mr Stamp was amazed to see so many children milling about in the playground. They were already changed into their soccer kit, waiting impatiently for him to arrive.

'Oh, well – here we go again,' he sighed.

After spending the day at home, Mr Stamp had turned up in his old tracksuit especially for the practice. He gave everyone a piece of equip-

27

ment to carry and then led the excited party onto the small park next to the school.

'Keen enough, at least, I'll say that for them,' he murmured as the youngsters warmed up by doing some stretching exercises.

Judging their actual footballing ability, however, was not going to be easy. The grass was so long in places as to be almost covering their socks. Mr Stamp laid out separate pitches with marker cones and then divided the players up into six-a-side teams.

'Don't bother about keeping the score,' he told them. 'Simply show me what you can do. I want to see how many superstars we have at the school.'

'Fraid there's only me, like,' said Harry, grinning.

The games began at a frantic pace, with all the players hoping to catch the teacher's eye.

Some of them did so for the wrong reasons, falling clumsily over their own feet or fouling others to get a kick of the ball. Mr Stamp wandered around the pitches, praising and encouraging their efforts, and occasionally swapping certain people from one team to another.

'Looks like he's trying to put the best players together,' Jack observed.

Callum nodded. 'Yeah, maybe,' he said and then pulled a face. 'Then again, maybe not. What's *she* doing here?'

Ellie had just been sent over to join in their game.

'About time,' Amy greeted her.

Ellie gave a shrug. 'Well, now I'm here, you won't get another touch.'

'Oh, yeah?' grinned Amy.

'Yeah.'

Ellie was wrong. The first thing she did was to trip her friend up as Amy tried to dribble past her. Amy insisted on taking the free-kick herself, despite protests from Callum, but moments later he was glad to have lost the argument.

Amy drilled the kick low and hard, giving Harry no chance of making a save as the ball

clipped a cone on its way in.

'Huh!' Harry grunted in dismay. 'Lucky, like, that was.'

'No luck,' Amy retorted. 'Just skill!'

That strike was soon cancelled out at the other end, but nobody was able to claim the credit for this one. As the ball trickled loose from a goalmouth scramble, it suddenly picked up pace and slithered past a defender who was guarding the line.

'Wicked spin!' cried Rajesh. 'Who scored it?'

'The invisible man!' laughed his twin brother, Dinesh.

Mr Stamp didn't see that incident and, in the gathering gloom, he also missed another strange goal on the neighbouring pitch.

'What happened?' he asked, as the bemused players were about to restart their game.

'Er, not exactly sure, Mr Stamp,' said one of them hesitantly. 'This girl sort of popped up out of nowhere and lashed the ball in.'

'Which girl?'

They all looked blank, as if suffering from a collective lapse of memory.

'Did she have red hair?'

'Yeah, think she did,' said a defender, scratching his head. 'And she'd got some dead old, tatty gear on.'

Mr Stamp realized there was no point in pursuing the questioning. He gave up and signalled the end of the session.

'Are you going to choose a squad, Mr Stamp?' asked Callum.

'I'll think about it,' the teacher replied. 'I'm not making any promises, but I don't mind giving you all the chance to play a bit of extra soccer. We'll have another practice next week for anyone who wants to come along.'

He was hoping to see at least one fresh face in particular.

Mr Stamp was not disappointed.

'Are you new to the school?' he asked the frail-looking girl who was perched on one of the cones while the other players were warming up.

Her reply was barely above a whisper.

'*Been here a long time*,' she said, pushing a wisp of red hair out of her eyes.

Mr Stamp didn't quite pick up her words but took the shake of her head to mean no.

'Right, well, you can play in Jack's team,' he told her, deciding on impulse to include her in the main game. 'What's your name?'

'*Victoria.*'

'Sorry – you'll have to speak a little louder.'

'*Victoria*,' she repeated with an effort.

The news didn't really surprise him, remembering the final name on his list. 'Right, Victoria, which position do you like best?'

She shrugged again. '*Don't mind.*'

He regarded her slim build, hidden beneath her rather baggy kit. 'Well, you look as if you might be able to run fast,' he said, handing her a blue training bib. 'Have a go on the wing.'

Victoria made little impact for the first ten minutes or so, just getting the odd touch of the ball, but then made her presence felt in spectacular style. Gaining possession on the right flank, she went on a weaving run goal-wards, so swift and light on her feet that three opponents were left trailing in her wake.

Harry came out towards her to narrow the

 32

shooting angle, but Victoria slipped the ball past him like a conjuring trick – now you see it, now you don't. The keeper dived down in her path only to grasp at thin air and Victoria was free to tap the ball home.

'Magic dribble!' cried Dinesh. 'You just ghosted past everybody.'

Victoria's thin face broke into a smile for the first time.

Later, while Mr Stamp was supervising the collection of equipment to take back to school, Victoria found herself surrounded.

'Ain't never seen you before.'

'Which class you in?'

'C'mon, tell us,' ordered Callum, resentful of the number of times she had made him look foolish during the game, knocking the ball through his legs or sending him the wrong way. 'You ain't in Freddie's class, are yer?'

'*Freddie?*' Her voice was like a gentle breeze, barely audible by anyone not right in front of her.

'She don't even know who Freddie is!' exclaimed Harry for the benefit of those who may not have heard.

'Yeah, Freddie,' Callum repeated. 'Mrs Fredericks, the deputy sheriff.'

Victoria was confused. She had no idea that their teacher's other nickname referred to the school's headmistress, Miss Marshall.

Jack came to her rescue. 'Leave her alone, you lot,' he said. 'What's the matter with you? Vicki's been brilliant.'

'Huh! Just 'cos she scored most of your goals,' Callum sneered.

'Well, that's exactly what we need in a school team. Somebody who can bang the ball in the back of the net.'

Harry pulled a face. 'Ain't even got any nets,' he lamented. 'Had to keep fetchin' the ball from the 'edge.'

'You shouldn't let so many shots in, then, should you?' Jack retorted, showing no sympathy. 'About time you stopped a few, if you want to be the school team goalie.'

 34

The group's attention switched from Victoria to a lively debate about who might be in the squad if Mr Stamp managed to arrange a match.

'How many girls d'yer reckon Stampy would pick?' said Rajesh.

'None, I hope,' grunted Callum.

'Come off it, Cally,' Jack grinned. 'There's Amy and Ellie for a start – and now we've got Vicki as well . . .'

He trailed off as he glanced round to find that Victoria had disappeared.

'Where's she gone to?' he asked, puzzled. 'She was standing there only a minute ago.'

'Bet she nipped off quick, like, so she don't 'ave to carry 'owt,' Harry cackled. 'C'mon, let's do the same.'

They left the park at a steady jog but the only ones to catch sight of the mysterious new striker were Amy and Ellie. The girls reached the playground just in time to see Victoria enter the building site. To their utter astonishment, she seemed to pass right through the safety fence, drift over the mounds of rubble and then fade from view.

An icy shiver snaked down Ellie's spine.

35

'Where . . . where did she go?'

Amy was in no state to reply. She stood rooted to the spot, open-mouthed, gawping at the empty space where Victoria had vanished.

4 CAN'T PLAY

Victoria did not reappear until the next practice session.

Mr Stamp hadn't been into school over the past week and knew nothing of her absence. 'Good news!' he announced when the footballers reached the park. 'I've organized a friendly game for you on Saturday.'

'Who's it against?' Callum interrupted, forgetting his manners.

Mr Stamp let it pass. 'The new school on the other side of town, Green Lane Primary,' he explained. 'They want to play an eleven-a-side match.'

'Is it at their place, Mr Stamp?' asked Jack.

'I'm afraid it has to be. We won't be able to get any suitable pitch here sorted out in time.'

'Have you picked the team yet, Mr Stamp?' Amy put in.

The teacher smiled but he sensed what the real question was behind it. 'No, but rest assured there will be some girls in it,' he replied – to her obvious satisfaction and Callum's barely concealed snort of disgust. 'I'll be letting you know who's playing during this practice so let's get cracking.'

As the children prepared for action, Mr Stamp felt a gentle tug at the sleeve of his tracksuit. He looked round to find Victoria behind him, white-faced.

'What's the matter?' he asked. 'Hope you're not feeling ill. We need you for the game.'

She seemed to turn even paler. *'Can't play,'* she whispered.

'Sorry, you'll have to speak up a bit. What did you say?'

'Can't play,' she sighed, shaking her head for added effect.

'What, on Saturday, you mean?'

Victoria nodded.

Now it was his turn to sigh. 'Oh, dear! I was relying on you to score a goal or two for us. Are you going somewhere?'

She shook her head again – this time more sadly, it seemed. *'Have to stay here,'* she murmured.

'You have to stay here?' he repeated to make sure he'd heard correctly. 'What do you mean? Why's that?'

She gave a slight shrug. *'Can't go,'* was all she could say by way of an excuse and he had to accept it at that.

'Well, that *is* a shame,' he said in genuine disappointment. 'Looks like we'll just have to try and manage without you, then, somehow.'

Playing on the left-wing in a full-scale practice game, Victoria was a shadow of her former self. Only once did she manage to get the better of Owen, her marker. Feinting to take the ball on the outside of the full-back, Victoria dummied inside, throwing Owen off-balance, and made for goal. Harry dashed out to meet her, but instead of dribbling round him, she ballooned the ball high and wide.

'Made yer panic,' Harry grinned.

Victoria retreated to the wing where Owen made sure she didn't escape his shackles again.

'Well done,' Mr Stamp praised the defender when he easily beat Victoria to the ball and cleared it upfield to end another attack. 'Best I've seen you play today.'

'Does that mean I'm in the team, Mr Stamp?'

'You are indeed.'

Owen jumped up and punched the air in

delight. 'YEEESSS!!!' he shrieked – so loudly that everyone else stopped playing.

Mr Stamp took the opportunity to name the squad of thirteen, with Jack as captain.

'Victoria would have been included, too, but unfortunately she's not available,' he said, peering around the group for her in vain. 'Where is she, anyway? She wasn't looking too well.'

'Like death warmed up,' muttered Amy under her breath.

'Bet she's gone home sulkin' 'cos she hardly had a kick,' Callum gloated, unaware of the furtive glance exchanged between Amy and Ellie.

As the game continued without Victoria, the two girls had a chance to speak in the middle of the pitch.

'She's good at disappearin' tricks, ain't she, our Victoria?' Ellie said, frowning. 'How d'yer think she does it?'

'Dunno, but she's even missing from the registers,' Amy replied. 'Got sent round the classes today to collect 'em all up and I checked. Couldn't see her name anywhere.'

'Well weird, all this, eh?' Ellie murmured.

Amy nodded. 'Yeah – spooky!'

 41

'Pity Vicki can't play tomorrow,' Jack said, gazing into the building site.

The boys' game of football in the playground had been suspended for the usual reason – lost ball. Frustratingly, they knew exactly where it was. They could see it sitting on a pile of soil on the other side of the metal fence.

Callum gave a snort of derision. 'She can't play at all, full stop,' he said. 'Don't rate her.'

'Why not? What about those goals she scored the other week.'

'Just luck. Anybody can score in practices.'

'*You* can't,' Jack taunted him.

'Yeah, well, I'm not a striker, am I? My job is to stop others scorin'.'

'You didn't do a very good job that day. She ran rings round you.'

'Rubbish!'

'C'mon, admit it. Vicki's a natural goalscorer.'

Callum smirked. 'You're always stickin' up for her. You fancy her or summat?'

'Course not,' Jack retorted. 'Just saying we'll miss her, that's all.'

'Don't think she'd have been playing, anyway,' Owen chipped in. 'Must be away. Not seen her around, have you?'

'You lot *ever* seen her around?'

The follow-up question came from Ellie, leaning against a wall nearby with Amy and eavesdropping on their conversation.

'What do you mean?' Jack demanded.

'I mean, you ever seen her at school, apart from playin' soccer?'

'Well, guess not, now you mention it,' Jack admitted in surprise.

'Didn't think so,' Ellie said smugly.

'So what yer gettin' at?' Callum muttered. 'You sayin' she doesn't actually come to this school?'

'Might have done at one time, maybe.'

'When?'

Ellie shrugged. 'Dunno. I'm no good at history.'

Jack lost his patience. 'Look, if you've got

 43

something to say, then just say it or belt up.'

It was Amy who said it.

'We reckon Victoria don't really exist.'

'What's that supposed to mean?' Jack replied in exasperation.

'We reckon she's some sort of ghost!'

That statement was a real conversation stopper. It took the boys a little time to recover from it.

'*Ghost!*' exclaimed Callum in stunned disbelief. 'You two must be even more stupid than we thought.'

Amy pulled a face at him. 'Call it what you like. How about phantom?'

'Yeah,' said Ellie in support. 'Victoria – the phantom footballer!'

5 FIRST MATCH

The following morning, it perhaps wasn't surprising that the minds of the footballers were not fully focused on the game.

Mr Stamp, however, was oblivious to the rumours about Victoria that had quickly spread through the school.

'Get a grip, Bradgate!' he called out from the touchline in exasperation. 'You're just not with it today.'

Poor marking from a corner had cost them dear. Harry was beaten for the second time in ten minutes by a close-range header and the goalkeeper wasn't slow to complain.

'Who's supposed to be pickin' up that big kid?' he yelled.

'Don't look at me,' Callum scowled. 'I was coverin' the number eight.'

'I was guarding the post,' added Dinesh before anybody could point the finger of blame towards him.

The captain put a stop to the arguing.

'Nothing we can do about it now,' Jack stated. 'Fact is, we're 2–0 down and we've hardly been in their half yet. C'mon, let's get at 'em!'

Jack rolled up his sleeves and tried to lead by example, crunching into a tackle to win possession and driving Bradgate forward from midfield. The players responded well. Not only did they give the Green Lane keeper his first touch of the ball, but Rajesh rattled the crossbar too with a fierce volley.

It wasn't enough, though, to knock the strong home team out of their stride for long. The Greens managed to regain control of the game and doubled the score before half-time. If it

46

hadn't been for two excellent stops by Harry, the situation would have been even more embarrassing.

When the referee blew for the brief interval, the Bradgate players trailed slowly towards their teacher.

Jack was the first to speak. 'We're playing rubbish,' he admitted.

'Well, you're certainly not playing like a team, that's for sure,' sighed Mr Stamp. 'Maybe that's expecting too much first time out.'

'But we're better than this,' the captain insisted.

'Yes, I like to think you are or I'd not have arranged this game for you.'

The teacher gazed at the dejected figures grouped around him in their blue and white quartered shirts. The school caretaker had found the faded soccer kit that week up in the attic of the old building, untouched since Mr Stamp had retired.

'I know this kit may not exactly be the height of fashion for you youngsters nowadays, but be proud to wear the school colours,' he urged. 'The last team to wear it won the league and cup double.'

Mr Stamp took the opportunity to make two substitutions and a few other positional changes for the second half before offering a final piece of encouragement.

'Just go and do your best,' he told them. 'Nobody can ask for more than that, whatever the result.'

The transformation in the game was remarkable. It might have been because Green Lane were trying out some reserves, but Mr Stamp liked to think it was mostly due to a vast improvement in his own players' attitude.

The concentration level was much better, the work rate was higher and they actually showed they could produce some decent football.

The first goal that Bradgate scored was the result of great skill by Amy. She controlled a lofted pass from Owen on her chest, played a one-two exchange with Rajesh, and then tucked the ball into the corner of the net.

4–1

It was Amy who nearly scored the second too. Her strike from the edge of the area rebounded from a post and the ball was lashed back past the helpless goalie by the captain himself.

4–2

To their credit, the Greens recovered well from the shock of conceding those two goals. They began to mount some dangerous attacks of their own again but met much sterner resistance. The Bradgate defence was now better organized and the visitors took inspiration from a couple of strong challenges by Callum and another fine save by Harry, high to his right.

Ellie also scooped the ball off the line in a goalmouth scramble, and from her clearance upfield

 49

Bradgate scored a third. Rajesh sprinted past the last defender and dribbled the ball round the keeper before slotting it home.

4–3

Sadly, that was as good as it got. With time running out, Bradgate pressed forward with increasing desperation in search of the equalizer and were caught on the break.

A long cross-field pass that switched play from one side of the pitch to the other found Owen outnumbered, having to cover two attackers. He chose the wrong one. The Greens' winger was left with a clear run to goal and he was cool enough to steer the ball wide of the advancing Harry into the net.

5–3

'A good fightback by your team,' the referee said to Mr Stamp after the final whistle. 'We must have a return match at your place soon.'

'Aye, if we can get a pitch marked out,' Mr Stamp replied. 'I was pleased with the spirit we showed second half.'

Jack overheard the teacher's comment. 'If Amy and Ellie are right,' he murmured to himself, 'we might well have even more spirit in the side when Vicki plays . . .'

6 PENALTY PRACTICE

'Hard luck, Victoria!' Mr Stamp called out. 'Deserved a goal.'

The winger's low shot had beaten Harry's full-length dive, leaving the keeper mightily relieved to see it skim wide of the cone.

Victoria had turned up again – or *materialized*, as Amy now termed her sudden appearances – right on cue, in time for the soccer squad's next practice session on the park.

 51

'How *can* she be a ghost?' Callum scoffed while waiting for the ball to come back into play. 'She's solid enough all right – and I should know. I've kicked her a few times.'

'Me too,' laughed Owen. 'And she's kicked us back!'

'Yeah, right. Bet them girls are just bein' catty about her.'

'But why is she never at school?'

'Perhaps she's got schoolitis,' Callum said with a shrug. 'Y'know, fear of school or summat like that.'

Owen was still grinning. 'She's sure good at playing truant, I'll say that for her. Even better than she is at playing football!'

The defenders had to break off their chat as Harry's weak clearance landed at Jack's feet. The captain shaped to knock the ball out to the right wing, but then swept a well-disguised pass out to the left instead.

With Owen caught out of position, Victoria made the most of the space that she now enjoyed, running so fluently with the ball that it seemed to Mr Stamp as if her feet barely touched the ground. The grass was so long, however, it was difficult to tell.

Harry was expecting another angled shot, but Victoria's lofted centre took the keeper by surprise. He was in no position to deal with it and the unmarked Amy headed the ball into the goal.

The scorer ran across to Victoria and slapped her hard on the back by way of thanks.

'*Ow!*' she squealed.

Amy smirked. 'Just testing. Wanted to see how real you were.'

Before Victoria could respond, the game was underway again. Rajesh won possession of the ball with a bone-jarring challenge on his twin and then laid it forward to Jack.

'Did you have to go in so hard?' Dinesh complained as Rajesh pulled him up onto his feet.

'Only 'cos it was you!' Rajesh chuckled, running off.

By the time Dinesh limped back to help in defence, the attackers had been awarded a corner. Rajesh tapped it short to Victoria, whose progress goalwards was halted rather crudely by Dinesh. Frustrated at not being able to seek immediate revenge on Rajesh, he stuck out a leg and tripped Victoria instead as she tried to dribble past him.

 53

'Penalty!' appealed Jack.

'Well, yes, I suppose it would be if we had a penalty area,' Mr Stamp agreed. 'But perhaps this is a good chance to practise penalties in case we ever get one in a proper match.'

He took a number of paces from the goal-line to decide where the penalty spot should be and then asked for volunteers. Half a dozen players raised their hands, including Victoria.

'You take the first one, seeing as it was you who got fouled,' Mr Stamp told her. 'Don't worry if you miss. It's only a practice.'

Victoria had no intention of missing and he never really doubted that she would. The girl had a cold, almost cruel look in her eye that might turn any goalkeeper to stone. It even sent a little shiver down his own spine.

Whether it was the harsh stare or the little jink in her run-up that mesmerised Harry wasn't certain, but the keeper seemed rooted to the spot as the ball whistled past him.

'On yer bike, Harry!' Callum cackled. 'Go and fetch it.'

Without a net behind him to snare the ball, Harry spent most of the next quarter of an hour retrieving the ball from the hedge. Most of the

    54

shots went in, a few sailed wide or high and he even managed to block some of them to save himself extra treks.

'OK, well done, everybody,' Mr Stamp called out when Jack blasted the ball past the goalie again. 'It's getting a bit too dark for poor Harry to see, I think. Time to go home.'

As the equipment was gathered up, Amy seized hold of Victoria's arm. 'Wait a minute, you,' she ordered. 'Don't want to let you have a chance for another of your vanishing acts. Just where is your home?'

Victoria tried to pull free without success and gave up. Ellie was also standing guard beside her.

'Well, you heard,' hissed Ellie. 'Where d'yer live?'

Amy gave a snort. 'Not sure *live* is quite the right word for a ghost!'

Victoria's face drained of whatever little colour it had. '*You are hurting me,*' she complained.

'Huh! Didn't know that *ghosts* could feel pain,' Amy sneered, tightening her grip even more. 'Tell us where you hang out and I'll let go.'

'*In the school,*' she whimpered.

'In the school?' Amy repeated, taken aback. 'Where exactly?'

'*In the attic.*'

'Stop messing about, you three,' Mr Stamp called to them. 'Come and help to carry some things back to school for a change.'

Amy released Victoria's arm. 'Just don't try any funny business,' she warned. 'We're watching you.'

'Um ... Mr Stamp?' began Ellie, picking

up a couple of footballs. 'You ever been in the school attic?'

'Whatever do you want to know that for?'

'Just wonderin' what was kept up there, y'know, apart from the soccer kit,' she said as an excuse. 'Might be a few things we could put on display for our Victorian project.'

'The kit's not *that* ancient!' Mr Stamp chuckled. 'I shouldn't think there's anything still left going back over a century. The attic must get cleared out every now and again.'

'Who by?'

'The caretaker, probably,' he said. 'Could be worth him going up there to have a check round, I suppose. You never know what might be found.'

'Or who,' Amy added meaningfully.

'Sorry?' said Mr Stamp, puzzled.

'Just teasing old Vic here,' said Amy, turning round to find there was no-one behind her.

Back at the school, having stored the equipment, Mr Stamp noticed the light was still on in the headteacher's office. He went to knock on the door.

'Come in.'

'Sorry to bother you, Miss Marshall,' Mr Stamp said as he entered. He explained Ellie's

 57

idea about searching the attic before mentioning the other matter on his mind. 'I was also wondering whether you can tell me anything about the thin, red-haired girl, Victoria, who comes to my soccer practices.'

Miss Marshall sat back in her chair behind the desk, looking puzzled. 'Victoria?' she mused. 'Whose class is she in?'

'Don't know, I'm afraid,' he admitted. 'She seems a strange sort of girl, somehow – a bit old-fashioned, the way she dresses and speaks. She's not really like the other kids at all.'

Miss Marshall shook her head. 'I can't think who this girl might be. We don't have a Victoria in the top juniors. What's her surname?'

'That's another odd thing,' he replied. 'She signed the notice I put up as Victoria Bradgate.'

'We certainly don't have anybody by that name in the school,' said the headteacher, grimacing. 'I'm beginning to think this *Victoria* is having a joke at your expense. I shall make a point of finding out just who she is and then have a very firm word with her.'

As Mr Stamp left the building, something

58
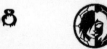

made him look upwards. He seemed to catch a fleeting glimpse of a face at the attic window.

'Must be seeing things,' he muttered, rubbing his eyes wearily. 'For a moment, I could have sworn that was Victoria up there . . .'

7 HOME, SWEET HOME

'There!' exclaimed Mr Stamp. 'What do you think of that, then?'

'Wicked!'

'Magic!'

The footballers gazed in astonishment at the park's freshly cut grass and the white markings of a soccer pitch. It even had goalposts set up.

'How did you manage all this, Mr Stamp?' Jack grinned.

'Contacts,' he beamed, tapping his nose in conspiracy. 'I didn't work at the school for years without getting to know a few people. Just picked up the phone last week and called in a couple of favours.'

'Fantastic! Our own pitch at last!' enthused the captain. 'Now we can take on Green Lane again.'

'Already arranged for Saturday,' Mr Stamp told them, chuckling. 'Borrowed some nets, too, for the game.'

The squad only had time for a short practice session in the fading light and they concentrated on set-piece moves at corners and free-kicks.

'Make yourselves hard to mark,' the teacher urged the main strikers, Amy, Victoria, Rajesh and a tall, fair-haired lad called Jordan. 'Don't just stand still. Dodge about and look for spaces.'

They didn't create as many clear-cut chances as Mr Stamp would have wished, although that was more due to good defending than the failings of the attackers. Any ball that did get past the tight marking usually ran harmlessly out of play or ended up in Harry's safe hands.

 62

He only conceded two goals, the second of which gave Mr Stamp cause for optimism about the outcome of the match itself.

Rajesh and Jordan swapped neat passes to set Amy free and she chipped the ball into the penalty area, catching Harry off his line. He back-pedalled furiously and lunged upwards, just managing to tip the ball onto the crossbar. The keeper was in no position, however, to deal with the rebound. Stranded on the ground, he could only watch Victoria pounce on the loose ball and tap it into the goal.

Mr Stamp gathered everybody around him at the end to name the team for Saturday. 'It's a ten o'clock kick-off so I want you at school by half past nine. Anyone got a problem with that?'

He looked at Victoria, but she met his gaze and shook her head.

'Reckon *she* might be here already,' Amy murmured under her breath.

'Good,' he continued. 'Right, so let's hope we can turn the tables on the Greens at home. They haven't yet come across our secret weapon.'

The other players were left in no doubt as to what – or to whom – Mr Stamp was referring. The trouble was, Victoria remained just as much of a mystery to them too.

Amy kept close to her all the way back to school, trailing behind the rest of the group. 'What's it like, then, being up in that dark attic on your own?'

Victoria ignored the taunt.

'Bit scary, I'd reckon,' Amy persisted, trying to goad Victoria into a response. 'Mind you, don't suppose someone like you is afraid of nasty creepie-crawlies – or even *ghosties* . . .'

Victoria suddenly took off at a run, catching her tormentor by surprise. Hampered by the cone that she was carrying, Amy gave chase, but lost sight of Victoria round a corner of the playground.

Amy came to a halt by the metal fence. 'Huh! Gone to ground again, have you?' she muttered, staring through the grille at the muddy building site. 'Home, sweet home!'

Bradgate enjoyed the best possible start to the match. Less than thirty seconds after the kick-off, Amy fired her team into a 1–0 lead.

Jack swept a long pass out to Victoria on the wing and her speed off the mark left the Greens' full-back stumbling in her wake. She cut inside towards goal to draw the keeper out of position before sliding the ball perfectly into the path of the onrushing Amy. The striker steadied herself and then took great delight in smashing the ball high into the roof of the net.

Mr Stamp wished he could join in the applause of the spectators lining the pitch. As referee, however, he had to content himself with a few words of praise as the players jogged back towards the centre-circle.

'Good goal, Amy,' he said, remembering her name for once.

'Couldn't miss,' she admitted, grinning. 'Old Vic just left them for dead!'

He smiled. 'Aye, they know all about our little secret weapon now.'

'That's more than we do,' Amy said to herself as Mr Stamp moved across to Victoria.

'Well done,' he called out. 'Keep it up.'

'Can't – not for long now. Thank you.'

He thought he must have misheard Victoria's response. She'd made it sound like she was even thanking him for letting her play – as if this would be her last game.

Mr Stamp was still puzzling over her words when Rajesh squandered a good chance to put Bradgate two goals in front, hooking the ball wide from close range.

The Greens made the most of their lucky escape. A minute later, they broke away out of defence and caused Harry to demonstrate the Jekyll-and-Hyde nature of his goalkeeping.

He raced forward to make a brave block at the feet of the burly number nine and, as the ball ran free, recovered in time to face the follow-up shot from a second attacker. The ball was hit straight at him, but Harry somehow let it squirm through his fingers and between his legs into the goal.

After such an explosive start, the game settled down for a while with neither side able to get on top. Most of the action took place in midfield and the two keepers had so little to do they could almost have leant on a post and read a couple of chapters of their library book.

Just when it began to look as though the stalemate would last until half-time, the Greens went ahead. Nobody was to blame. It was simply a very good move and a well-struck volley, which zoomed past the helpless Harry into the back of the net.

The goalie still felt he had to apologize at the break. 'Soz, guys,' he muttered sheepishly. 'Dunno how that first one went in, like.'

'Never mind. These things happen in football,' sighed Mr Stamp. 'You don't deserve to be 2–1 down, team, but at least that's a lot better than last time. Now go and show everybody how you can really play.'

As the second half kicked off, the crowd had increased by two more people – and their unexpected arrival did not go unnoticed for long.

'Amazing!' cried Owen, pointing them out. 'Look who's here.'

'Marshall and the deputy-sheriff!' gasped Dinesh. 'Never thought they'd come and watch us play football.'

Dinesh was both right and wrong. The two teachers were on a different mission altogether.

Mr Stamp also mistook their intentions. 'Nice to see you supporting the team,' he greeted them when the ball went out of play for a throw-in nearby.

'We're not here for that,' said Miss Marshall, frowning. 'We want to have a good look at that Victoria girl.'

'Is that her on the far side?' asked Mrs Fredericks.

'Well, yes . . .' began Mr Stamp, 'but why . . .?'

Mrs Fredericks cut him off. 'I've never seen her before,' she stated flatly. 'She certainly isn't one of our pupils.'

'And perhaps she never was,' added the head-teacher, ashen-faced.

8 PENALTY!

'Great save, Harry!' cried Jack after the goalkeeper held on to a stinging shot at full stretch. 'That's kept us in the game.'

Only Miss Marshall and Mrs Fredericks failed to appreciate Harry's heroics. They were striding around the pitch to get a closer look at the red-haired girl in the number eleven blue and white quartered shirt.

The next time Victoria received the ball,

she treated everyone to a wonderful display of her dribbling skills. The full-back was almost turned inside-out by her trickery, losing his balance as Victoria sold him a dummy with a swift change of direction.

She dodged past the clumsy challenge of another defender and then glanced up to select her target – Jordan. The ball curled into the goalmouth and the big striker leapt high at the far post to head it powerfully past the keeper into the net.

'The equalizer!' he yelled, arms raised in delight. 'C'mon, let's grab that winner now. We can do it.'

Jordan was right. Another goal straightaway might well have set Bradgate on the road to victory, but their more experienced opponents managed to keep them at bay – with a little help from the woodwork when Jack clattered a shot against the post.

'What's your name, girl?'

The sharp voice made Victoria jump. She had wandered over near the touchline, waiting for the ball to come her way again, as the Greens forced Bradgate back into their own half for a while.

'Well, answer me,' snapped Miss Marshall. 'Who are you?'

'*Victoria*,' she whispered.

'Speak up, girl. What did you say?'

'*Victoria, Miss.*'

'What's your full name?' demanded Mrs Fredericks.

Victoria didn't answer.

'Is it Bradgate?'

'*Yes, Miss.*'

Even though they had been half expecting confirmation of the girl's identity, it still didn't lessen the shock.

The interrogation ended as the ball was cleared and Victoria gave chase to win possession. Her speed changed defence into attack in an instant. Victoria sprinted half the length of the field, outpacing both friend and foe, until only the final defender barred her path to goal. It was no contest. She waltzed round him and was about to shoot when he yanked her off-balance by the shirt collar.

'Penalty!' chorused the Bradgate players and Mr Stamp had no option but to blow his whistle and point to the spot.

'Who's going to take it?' asked Jack, hoping

 73

the teacher would say it was the captain's responsibility.

'Um, I think that's already been decided,' Mr Stamp replied, nodding towards Victoria. She was calmly settling the ball in position, oblivious to anyone else's claims.

'Huh! She'd better not miss or I'll kill her,' muttered Amy.

'Bit late for that!' Ellie grinned, making them both snigger.

The keeper tried to distract the kicker, flapping his arms and jumping up and down on the line as if he were about to take off. His wild antics were all to no avail. Victoria wrong-footed him with a subtle dip of her shoulder at the last moment, stroking the ball into the opposite corner of the goal to put Bradgate 3–2 ahead.

The scorer vanished from view under a mob of

celebrating teammates, who sensed that the game was now theirs. It was only as the group broke up that Mr Stamp realized that Victoria was no longer anywhere to be seen.

The teachers on the touchline were equally dumbfounded by her disappearance, staring around the park in confusion. Only the players seemed relatively unconcerned. Mr Stamp brought on a substitute to replace the missing star for the last few minutes of the match, but the Greens had little heart or energy left to stage a fightback. They were a beaten side.

'We've won!' Jack exclaimed, punching the air at the final whistle. 'What a game!'

As the players began to make their way back towards the school, Miss Marshall marched onto the pitch to confront Mr Stamp.

'Have you *any* idea where that Victoria went to?'

He made a helpless gesture with his hands. 'Sorry, it's a complete mystery to me as well.'

'It's high time it was solved,' she said with determination. 'I want you to come into my office as soon as you can. We've got something to show you.'

A quarter of an hour later, after checking the

 75

cloakrooms were clear, Mr Stamp knocked on the office door. As he entered the room, Miss Marshall pointed to a dusty pile of books on her desk.

'The caretaker discovered several boxes of these when he searched the attic yesterday,' she told him.

'What are they?'

'Old log books going right back to the mid-nineteenth century when Lord Bradgate founded the school.'

'That's even before my time,' said Mr Stamp, attempting a weak joke to hide his own foreboding about what he might be going to learn.

Mrs Fredericks took over. 'We haven't had a chance to go through them properly yet, but we've already come across several references to a girl known as Victoria Bradgate,' she explained. 'She was an orphan child, born in the workhouse, and named after the local lord.'

'Coincidence, surely,' he said.

'We just don't know what to think,' sighed Miss Marshall. 'According to these records, the poor girl never actually attended this school. She went missing, presumed dead, while it was being built, but her restless spirit – or whatever we choose to call it – can't stay away from the place.'

'How do you mean?'

'It – she – keeps coming back,' said the head-teacher. 'Every fifty years. And now, it would seem, here she is again.'

9 HIDE AND SEEK

'We shouldn't be doin' this,' Ellie hissed. 'We'll get done if we're caught.'

'Just belt up, will you,' Amy retorted as they reached the top of the stairs. 'Nobody will see us. Old Stampy's with Freddie in Marshall's office and the caretaker's busy cleaning up all the mess in the cloakrooms.'

'How d'yer know we can get up into the attic?'

'Saw the ladder in position when I nipped into

class to get a book out my desk. Caretaker must've been up there while we were playing the match.'

'What for?'

'How should I know?' Amy snapped. 'Perhaps he was getting Victoria's lunch ready.'

'No need to be sarky.'

'Well, stop asking so many stupid questions. Wish I hadn't got you to come with me now.'

'So do I,' Ellie muttered under her breath.

'Just keep a look out, OK? That's all you need do while I have a quick butcher's.'

'Have you got a torch?'

'That's another stupid question,' Amy said impatiently. 'Course I ain't. D'yer think I carry a torch around with me?'

'So how you gonna see?'

Amy sighed. 'Bound to be a light switch some-where,' she said as they sneaked along the main corridor.

'Be quick,' Ellie urged. 'Don't mess about up there for ages.'

'Depends what I find,' Amy grinned, placing a foot on the bottom rung of the ladder. 'Or *who* I find!'

Amy stared into the dark attic opening in the

high ceiling, took a deep breath and then stepped onto the next rung. She hadn't cared to admit to Ellie that she had no real head for heights. She didn't even much like using the climbing frames in P.E. lessons.

Clinging tightly to the sides of the ladder, Amy forced herself upwards, step after shaky step, until she was able to poke her head through the hatchway and peer into the gloom. It was only as she loosened her grip to feel around for a light switch that a voice whispered in her ear.

'What are you doing here?'

Amy gave a shriek of surprise and jerked backwards. If it hadn't been for a hand grabbing hold of her coat collar, she would have toppled off the ladder.

'So what do you want us to do?' asked Amy when they stopped by the deserted building site.

'*Follow me.*'

'Yeah, we've already done that. Where to now?'

Victoria kicked an old football from the attic over the fence. '*There!*'

'Oh, no,' Ellie refused. 'We've come with you to here, like you asked, but no further.'

'She *has* just saved my life,' Amy reminded her. 'And now she wants our help.'

'Aren't you forgettin' somethin'?'

'What?'

'We can't just walk through this fence like she can.'

'Right – good point,' Amy conceded reluctantly.

Ellie turned to confront Victoria. 'Look,' she began, 'just what is it exactly that you're so keen to show us?'

'*My grave.*'

If that answer stunned the girls into silence, Victoria's next statement made them stare at her in horror.

'*Got buried alive.*'

It was some seconds before Amy felt able to speak.

'Er . . . how did it happen?' she croaked.

 82

'*Playing a game*,' Victoria whispered. '*Hide and seek*.'

'When was this?'

She gave a little shrug. '*When school was built*.'

Amy gasped. 'That's a hundred and fifty years ago!'

Victoria showed no reaction, as if the passage of time meant little to her. '*Fell into hole*,' she continued. '*All went dark*.'

'You must've got knocked out and then covered over without anyone realizing,' murmured Amy, suppressing a shudder at the thought of such a terrible fate.

'Reckon you won that game all right,' Ellie added, not knowing what else to say. 'Nobody ever found you.'

To their surprise, Victoria actually smiled.

'*Till now*,' she said and repeated her request. '*Follow me*.'

They had no chance to respond. Victoria had already slipped through the metal barrier and was floating over the foundations of the new building. She turned to beckon to them and began to bend down as though she was about to pick up the ball. Then the figure, still dressed in

 83

soccer kit, slowly sank from sight altogether.

Although the girls had seen it happen before, they could still scarcely believe the evidence of their own eyes.

'This is crazy!' Amy exclaimed. 'How does she expect us to do that?'

'Well, I'm not even gonna try,' Ellie said defiantly.

'Suppose that's the least I can do,' Amy sighed. 'Just give it a try.'

Checking around to make sure nobody was watching, Amy attempted to climb over the fence, but it proved too high and awkward. She gave up and examined her scratched hands.

'Huh!' she grunted, cursing Victoria under her breath. 'Probably wants me to break my neck and join her!'

'If that was the case, she wouldn't have

stopped you fallin' off the ladder,' Ellie pointed out.

Amy started to search for any weak link in the barrier and found a small gap between two of the sections at the far end. After a lot of pushing and tugging, they made it just wide enough for her to squeeze through.

'Coming with me?' she said hopefully.

Ellie shook her head. 'Soz – I'll stay here on guard duty again.'

Amy began to tread gingerly across the uneven foundations towards the spot where Victoria had vanished. It would have been a tricky operation at the best of times and this was definitely not one of those. She twice lost her balance, wobbled and nearly toppled over.

Amy finally reached the ball and sat on the brickwork in relief, aware of the pounding of her heart. 'OK, so just what am I supposed to do now?' she panted, as if seeking spiritual guidance from beyond the grave.

She didn't expect an answer, but received one of a sort. Glancing into the hole beneath her feet, Amy saw an old football boot. She recognized it immediately. As she lifted it up, she touched something else poking through the soil

– something hard but brittle, with a jagged edge.

Amy pulled it out and brushed off the dirt, then held the object up into the light for a better look. It was only at that moment that she realized what she was actually holding.

'Uugh!' she cried in disgust. 'It's a piece of bone!'

'Watch out! Stampy's coming!'

The warning came too late. Ellie had been so busy following Amy's progress that she had failed to notice the teacher's approach until he was almost upon them.

Mr Stamp was taken by surprise too. Still mulling over what he'd just been told in the office, he was trudging back towards the park to take down the nets.

'Ellie? Why are you hanging around here?' he asked. 'You should be at home by now.'

As Ellie tried in vain to come up with some sort of answer, he looked through the fence and his mouth dropped open. The last thing he'd expected to see was a girl standing waist deep in a hole in the building site.

'Er, hello, Mr Stamp,' she faltered. 'It's only me, Amy.'

'What on earth are you doing in there? Don't

you know how dangerous it is?'

She said the first thing that came to mind. 'I was getting this ball back.'

'You should have left it,' he told her, his concern for the girl's safety overriding his anger. 'Can you get out or are you stuck?'

'I'm OK, Mr Stamp,' she assured him, 'but I think you'd better come and take a look at what I've just found . . .'

GHOST-SCRIPT

A *month later, during the Christmas holi-
days, four children are standing in front of
a new headstone in the town cemetery . . .*

'D'yer reckon she'll ever come back again, like?'
said Harry.

Jack shook his head. 'Shouldn't think so. Not
now she's had a funeral and got a proper grave
at last.'

'Her hauntin' days are over,' Ellie assured them, pointing to the headstone. 'Like it says on here. Victoria Bradgate – R.I.P.'

'Rest in peace,' Jack added.

'I know what them letters mean,' retorted Harry.

'More like *Rest in Pieces*, in her case,' Amy said with a grimace. 'She was just a load of old broken bones.'

'You only saw a bit of the skeleton,' Ellie said. 'Stampy got you straight out of that hole and then called the police.'

Amy shrugged. 'Yeah, well, she still wasn't a pretty sight.'

'Look who's talkin'!' smirked Harry. 'And you ain't even got the excuse of bein' buried all them years.'

Amy pulled the ugliest face that she could at him.

'See what I mean!' he laughed.

Jack sighed. 'At least we gave Vicki a good send off. It was great that some of her team-mates were allowed to carry her coffin into the church.'

'A nice touch by old Stampy, too, drapin' one of the kits over it,' Ellie reminded them. 'And what he said about her durin' the service.'

'What was it again?' Harry murmured, trying to recall the teacher's words. 'She'll soon be an angel flyin' down the wing in 'eaven's first eleven.'

'Somethin' like that,' Ellie nodded.

'It's best that Vicki went out at the top,' said Jack. 'Y'know, scoring the winning goal like she did. But we're going to miss her, no doubt about that.'

Harry bounced his football on the path next to the grave. 'C'mon, gang, we'd better get some practice in if we want to do well next term without our flyin' angel.'

'Yeah, got to prove we can manage without any help from above,' said Ellie.

'From up in the attic, you mean?' grinned Amy, giving the headstone a final farewell pat. 'Or from down below ground?'

They wandered thoughtfully away along the path towards the gate and the nearby park.

'Hey! I've just worked out what else R.I.P. can stand for,' Jack chuckled. 'Real Immortal Player!'

'Dunno about that,' Amy smiled. 'But we all know one thing about old Vic – she sure was dead good!'

THE END

ABOUT THE AUTHOR

Rob Childs was born and grew up in Derby. His childhood ambition was to become an England cricketer or footballer – preferably both! After university, however, he went into teaching and taught in primary and high schools in Leicestershire, where he now lives. Always interested in school sports, he coached school teams and clubs across a range of sports, and ran area representative teams in football, cricket and athletics.

Recognizing a need for sports fiction for young readers, he decided to have a go at writing such stories himself and now has more than seventy books to his name, including the popular *Soccer Mad* and *the County Cup* series, published by Corgi Yearling Books.

Rob has now left teaching in order to be able to write full-time. Married to Joy, a writer herself, Rob is also a keen photographer, providing many pictures for Joy's books and articles.

SOCCER SHOCKS
by Rob Childs

'What a way to end the season!'

The football season may be drawing to a close, but Luke Crawford – skipper, player-manager and coach of the Swillsby Swifts Sunday League team – is still full of running. . . when he's not tripping up over his own feet.

He's also still full of ideas and dreams. Luke's new sweeper system for the Swifts relies on the unpredictable talents of his Italian cousin Ricki, but will it be too late to save them from relegation? Luke would dearly love to win a medal in the school Cup Final, too, if only he's given the chance to get on the pitch.

One thing's for certain. With soccer-mad Luke on the loose, there are bound to be plenty of shocks in store for everyone before the final whistle blows. . .

The terrific climax to the bestselling SOCCER MAD series

0 440 864038

THE COUNTY CUP
by Rob Childs

Each year, schools from all over the county of
Medland take part in a great soccer tournament
– aiming to win the much-prized silver trophy,
the County Cup. Follow the fortunes of all the
teams as they battle to prove themselves the
top team in Medland in this super football
series that combines plenty of match action
with first-person comments, results, statistics
and team information.

Who will be the Champions?

The Quarter Championships
1. Cup Favourites
2. Cup Rivals
3. Cup Shocks
4. Cup Clashes

The Semi-Finals
5. Cup Glory
6. Cup Fever

The Final
7. Cup Winners

Available now from Corgi Yearling Books.

All Transworld titles are available by post from:

Bookpost
PO Box 29
Douglas
Isle Of Man IM99 1BQ

Tel: +44 (0) 1624 836000
Fax: +44 (0) 1624 837033
Internet http://www.bookpost.co.uk or e-mail:
bookshop@enterprise.net

Free postage and packing in the UK.
Overseas customers: allow £1 per book
(paperbacks) and £3 per book (hardbacks).